Praise for Dawn Van Beck's Children's Stories

"I'm over the moon thrilled that master storyteller Dawn Van Beck has ventured into writing children's books, too! With the same humor and heart that are at the core of her short stories, she's created the world of Lazy Lilly the Dachshund and her new BFF Tucker. So much fun!"

--- D. D. Scott, International Bestselling Author

Lazy Lilly and the Big Surprise

Written by

Dawn Van Beck

Illustrated by

Jenine Derix

First Electronic Edition: December 2019
First Print Edition: December 2019

eBook and Print Book Design & Formatting by
D. D. Scott's LetLoveGlow Author Services

*Dedicated to my sweet mother who,
by her example, fostered and nurtured my
love and compassion for animals
of all kinds.*

Once upon a time there lived a little doggy who had a velvet black coat, tan paws and brown eyes. She looked like a *L-O-N-G* hot dog, with short legs and soft ears that swung sideways when she walked.

When the doggy was two years old, she still didn't have a name. She had no place to live and no one to love her until Amanda, her new owner, brought her home to live with her.

Amanda named her Lilly.

Amanda tried for many months to play with Lilly but had no luck. When she tossed a ball, Lilly just watched it roll to a

stop. When she shook a toy for Tug of war, Lilly backed up, staring at her. Aside from sometimes zooming through the house at breakneck speed for no reason whatsoever, it was clear all Lilly wanted to do was…sleep.

Lilly loved to sleep! Sometimes she just rested, popping open one eye if she heard a noise. Other times, she would drift into a deep sleep and dream wild doggy dreams, letting out tiny whimpers or sometimes a growl.

One morning, Lilly heard a rustling in the kitchen. Jumping from her cozy bed, she ran to explore. After all, she never knew if and when Amanda might give her a second breakfast. With her ears flopping back and forth, Lilly yipped, trotting circles around Amanda's feet, hoping to have a morsel of whatever she was having.

"Wuff! Wuff!"

Unfortunately for Lilly, Amanda was only fetching her morning coffee before leaving for work. *Doggies don't drink coffee!*

"Be good today, my lazy pup, and don't fight with any of the neighbors when you go out your doggy door." Amanda patted the top of Lilly's head. "Oh—and I'm bringing home a surprise for you today!" Amanda turned, skipping out the door.

Lilly had no idea what Amanda's words meant, but they sounded good.

Crouching down, Lilly fixed her eyes on the door where Amanda disappeared until the rattle of the garage door stopped. Wandering over to the front window, she collapsed into her fuzzy bed. With a flip and twirl of her blanket, she twisted and turned until she was wrapped like a burrito. Of course, she left a tiny opening in the blanket for peeking out.

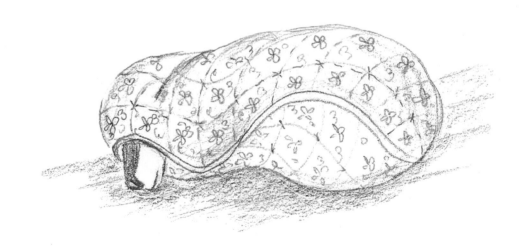

Lilly mashed her nose into the corner of her bed and…slept.

She napped most of the day. Occasionally, she peeked out windows or slurped some water. Every so often, she also trotted out to her backyard to bark at the neighbors. Lilly

liked to bark, a lot. Sometimes, she rolled over and over on the living room carpet like a log, and then…she napped some more.

Nestled inside her comfy blanket, Lilly snoozed for hours. Until…

A sharp twinge clawed at her belly. It was time for dinner. *How could that be?* Amanda wasn't home yet. It wasn't like her to be gone when Lilly's tummy was rumbling. *Where was she?*

Lilly sat up and peered out the window, waiting.

Just as she opened her jaw in a wide yawn, a clattering came from the garage. *What was that?* At the slam of a car door, she jumped. Tilting her head to the side as she lifted one paw, her ears popped up. *Could it be?* Scuffling to the kitchen, she barked at the loud grinding coming from beyond the laundry door. *Yes!* It was the garage door opening. Amanda was home again!

Lilly stood, swishing her tail back and forth like a windshield wiper. Amanda walked into the house balancing a box in her arms—a noisy box.

Lilly stood at attention with her tail straight up.

Shuffling, scratching and yipping came from inside the box.

Lilly stared at the box as Amanda reached

inside and pulled out a small, squeaking creature.

"This is your new little friend," Amanda said, setting the creature smack dab in front of Lilly.

Lilly backed up, tucking her tail under her body. "Wuff! Wuff! Wuff!"

"Arf! Arf! Arf!" The small critter barked right back.

Lilly glared as the critter scampered so fast, he tipped himself over. As he rolled around, Lilly discovered this was an itty-bitty puppy that looked L-O-N-G like her, except he was a little boy. He had big ears fluffed with fur. His coat was colored with gray and black swirls. Black speckles dotted his face. His stubby paws were soft, like mittens.

Lilly's eyes darted back and forth as she watched the puppy, wondering why he was in her house.

"Arf! Arf—arf—arf!"

Lilly had enough. A growl vibrated from deep within her chest. Turning away, she skedaddled to a nearby blanket and dove into it.

"It's gonna be okay, sweet girl. You'll see." Amanda patted the top of the blanket Lilly was buried under. "You and Tucker will be the best of friends."

Hmmm...the puppy's name is Tucker.

And Tucker loved to play! He loved to scoot, squirm, wiggle and romp...all the time. If he wasn't dumping over his food bowl with his plump paws, he was sailing through the house scattering papers everywhere. He attacked his toys until they were nothing but lumps of stuffing. Sometimes, he nipped at Amanda's ankles with his needle-sharp teeth, but she never scolded him because he was apparently so adorable. In fact, he always looked like he was smiling when he napped, which wasn't very often.

Lilly wanted nothing to do with Tucker.

He'd slobber on toys and drop them in front of her, but she'd turn away. He'd hop around

17

her food bowl when they were eating, but she ignored him. Sometimes, she even growled, warning him to leave her alone. He was a wild little puppy—and all Lilly wanted to do was sleep.

One day, Tucker was being an enormous pest. An even more enormous pest than normal. He zigged, zagged, zipped and jumped, determined to play with Lilly. Exhausted from trying to ignore him, Lilly tumbled into one of her beds and huffed.

Tucker sat in front of her with his tongue hanging out, wagging his tail. He released a playful growl, preparing to spring forward. Just as he waggled his hind end, Lilly noticed the bright, red ball lying in front of her bed.

It sure is round. It sure is red.

With a sudden pounce, Lilly sank her teeth into it. Giving the ball a powerful shake, she tossed it into the air, sending Tucker running. Much to her own surprise, Lilly flew from her bed and began chasing the bright red ball with Tucker.

Together, they batted the ball  back and forth,

to and fro, hither and yon. They rolled, bounced, yipped and yapped as they raced through the house bounding after the toy.

Amanda seemed so happy to see them finally playing with each other.

So began the first of many playdates between Lilly and Tucker. They chased

after squeaky stuffed animals, raced each other through the house, and charged after that bright red ball. Tucker had finally taught Lilly how to play.

He didn't know it yet, but she had a little something to teach him, too…

One lazy afternoon, Lilly watched Tucker's tummy rise and fall as he napped across the room in his own little bed. Always restless, he never slept too long. Tapping her tail, she sounded a quick bark, causing his head to pop up.

They stared at each other for a long moment before Lilly scooched herself over in her warm bed. Tucker smacked his fat paws across the floor, making his way closer. Finally, he stretched, shook himself and circled several times before climbing into Lilly's bed.

Nuzzling next to each other, they tucked their paws beneath them. As Tucker rested his nose in the blanket, Lilly licked the top of his puppy head. They curled into a tight ball, let out a huge sigh, and fell into a *D-E-E-P* sleep.

Lilly had finally taught Tucker something… the fine art of…sleeping.

THE END

Acknowledgements

Warm, heartfelt thanks to the following:

First, thanks to you, my reader. I'm truly honored you've chosen your valuable time to escape into my stories. Thanks to my friends, my family, and my writing tribe for your continual encouragement and inspiration. Thanks to my dear friend, Laura for sharing her huge heart with me for many years and for always cheering me on. Finally, to my Jeffrey, who always believes in me and paves the way for me to follow my dreams.

Note From the Author

I sincerely hope you've enjoyed reading my stories as much as I've enjoyed writing them. Also, I hope you come back for more! To be the first to hear of any new publications sign up for my mailing list at www.dawnvanbeck.com. Please be assured your email will never be shared, and you can unsubscribe at any time.

Hoping you will share your love of my stories with others . . . that's the best way for other readers to get to know me! If you've enjoyed what you've read, please leave a review on the site for the store from which you purchased it. Your efforts and support are so greatly appreciated.

Feel free to connect with me on:
https://www.dawnvanbeck.com
Facebook Dawn Van Beck
Pinterest Dawn Van Beck
Twitter @dawnvanbeck

Happy Reading!

About the Author

Hi there! Welcome to "me". I'm a writer, singer, child of God, and chocolate chip cookie connoisseur. I hold a degree in Human Resources with a concentration in Gerontology which has allowed me a rewarding career advocating for vulnerable senior adults. After transitioning out of my private Guardianship practice of several years, I now work alongside my husband with our moving business as well as put in some part-time hours at an Elder Law office . . . still advocating for seniors.

My love of all things writing began at an early age, pretending to be a librarian leading "story time" with my imaginary patrons. Over the years I've contributed to various publications including newsletters, magazines and theater pieces. My first official publication was in 1993 for the magazine "West Coast Woman", where I shared my experience of living with a Multiple Sclerosis diagnosis. Now, after years of dreaming, I'm finally publishing the dozens of short stories I've written as well as a children's picture book and working on wrapping up a Christian Romance novel.

I make my home in sunny Florida where I'm surrounded by a ridiculous number of writing journals and artisan coffee mugs. I love rummaging through antique shops, the arresting aroma of lavender, and I admit a quirky affinity for all things office supplies! Closer to my heart are bear hugs from my crazy husband, time spent with my adult children, and the companionship of Lilly, our feisty Daschund.

I believe we all have a voice and many things need to be said. What better way than to write stuff down? For me, writing is a way to express my thoughts of the world around me, to describe experiences that move my spirit, and to share how God meets me daily just as I am, with all my broken pieces. Join me as we journey together sharing short stories, devotions, miscellaneous musings and an occasional rant or two (or three).

Come, sit for a spell . . . I'll put the coffee on.

Books by Dawn Van Beck

Short Story Collections:
Autumn Love (Three Short & Sweet Romance Stories)
Holiday Moments (Holiday Short Stories)
More Coming in 2020!

Children's Picture Books:
Lazy Lilly and the Big Surprise

Christian Short Stories:
Child of Mine – *Coming Soon!*

Made in the USA
Columbia, SC
25 March 2023